GGERS and DUMPERS

Valerie Wilding • Maria Maddocks

Green Bananas

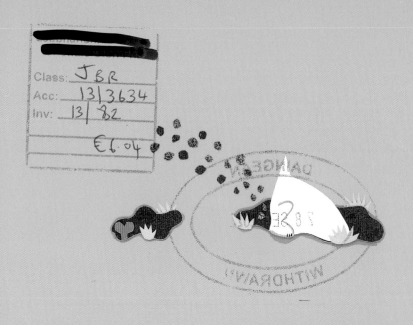

EGMONT

We bring stories to life

Book Band: Green

First published in Great Britain 2006
by Egmont UK Ltd.
239 Kensington High Street, London W8 6SA
Text copyright © Valerie Wilding 2006
Illustrations copyright © Maria Maddocks 2006
The author and illustrator have asserted their moral rights.
ISBN 978 1 4052 2230 3
10 9 8 7 6
A CIP catalogue record for this title is available from the British Library.
Printed in Singapore

Splosh!

Snap!

Dump!

For Julia and Mike – miss you loads
VW

For my family, with love.
Thank you for your encouragement,
love and support
MM

Splosh!

Leo had a new yellow digger.

It had big wheels and a shiny shovel.

'This is the best digger ever!' he said.

One morning, Ben came to play.

He brought his red dumper truck.

Wow!

'Wow! I like your digger!' said Ben.

'Can I have a go?'

'No,' said Leo. 'I've got a lot of

digging to do today.'

Leo drove his digger down the path.

He scooped up Curly's bone.

Gobble!
Gobble!

Curly had fun chasing the digger.

Ben got his truck and raced

after them!

Vroom! Vroom!

They raced round the roses.

They skidded round the tree.

'My digger's faster than your old truck,' said Leo.

'It's not,' said Ben. 'Watch!'

His truck chased the digger round

the sandpit.

'Look out!' yelled Leo. 'We're going

to crash!'

Look out!

They turned downhill.

Faster, faster . . .

Ugh!

SPLOSH!

They landed in a patch of mud.

'Look what you've done!' said Leo.

'My shiny digger isn't shiny

any more.'

'It wasn't me,' said Ben. 'You did it

yourself!'

'I didn't!' said Leo.

'You did!' said Ben.

'Boys!' said Mum.

'Come and have a lolly.'

17

They ate their lollies.

Leo was cross and Ben was cross.

They didn't say a word.

Snap!

'Let's wash your digger,' said Ben.

'We'll make it bright and shiny again.'

Leo held the hose and Ben turned on the tap.

First they washed the digger.

Then they washed the truck.

'Now you need a wash,' said Leo.

He squirted Ben!

23

Ben grabbed the hose

and squirted Leo.

Curly jumped up and pushed Ben

over, but – oh no!

Ben fell on Leo's digger.

SNAP! The shovel broke off.

Look what you've done!

Leo was so angry, he pushed Ben.

Ben pushed Leo back.

'I'm not playing with you any more,'

said Leo.

'I don't care,' said Ben, but he did really.

Leo tried to mend the shovel with tape, but it wouldn't stick.

He threw it on the floor.

'I can't fix it!' he shouted at Ben.

'It's ruined!'

Mum came in. 'What are you shouting for?' she asked.

'Ben broke my digger,' said Leo.

'I didn't mean to,' said Ben.

Sorry.

'Let's see,' said Mum. 'Perhaps the shovel just clips on.'

She pushed, she pulled, and – SNAP!

The digger was as good as new.

'Are you going to play with me?'

said Leo.

'Do you want me to?' said Ben.

Leo nodded.

He picked up the digger again.

Ben filled the dumper truck with

sand.

Dump!

After lunch, Mum said,

'Let's go to the park.'

'Do we have to?' said Leo.

'Oh, come on,' said Mum.

'It'll be fun.'

Leo drove a police car to the park.

Ben drove a spinning cement mixer.

Suddenly Ben crashed.

As Leo helped him up, he spied a

hole in the fence.

He looked through the hole.

'Wow!' said Leo. 'Come and see!'

'Diggers and trucks!' said Ben. 'Real digging and dumping!'

'I wonder what they're building,' said Mum.

At the park, Ben climbed on the jungle gym.

'I can see the diggers from here!' he yelled.

Leo climbed up beside him.

'So can I!' he cried. 'Those shovels scoop up lots of earth!'

They watched the diggers digging, and they watched the trucks dumping.

Look!

Leo and Ben ran to Mum.

'Can we go home?' they said.

Mum laughed. 'But we've only been here ten minutes!'

Let's go!

Leo and Ben wanted to get back to
their own digger and truck.

They hurried home.

43

They played with the digger and the truck again. But this time they played together. Dig, dig, dig! went Leo, as he scooped up sand.

Chug-a-lug! went the digger as Leo
drove it away. Swoosh! He tipped
the sand into Ben's truck.

Ben drove around the garden.

Vroom!

He dumped the sand on the path.

Dump! Dump! Dump!

'Let's do it again!' he said.

It's like a building site!

'Yes!' said Leo. 'But let's swap. You have my digger, and I'll have your truck!'

'I'll get some stones,' said Ben. 'This is fun!'

Swoosh!

When Ben's mum came to pick him up, she said, 'Can Leo come to Ben's house next week?'

'Oh, yes. Please!' Leo's mum said.